" 'The worst book ⸺ ⸺ was one I wrote myself,' writes Ron Kolm. Hapless junkies, dead-end jobs, failed marriages are all part of the landscape in his stories and, despite the misery of lives whose monotony is broken only by crisis, I laugh out loud. One, because he is damned funny and two, because wherever he goes I have wandered there as well. And, like the author, survived to tell the tale."
— Puma Perl is the author of *knuckle tattoos,* and *Retrograde*, and creator of Puma Perl's Pandemonium, which brings together spoken word and rock and roll

"Ron Kolm has the memory of Anthony Powell, the descriptive powers of Elizabeth Bishop and the sex-mad *joie de vivre* of Andrei Codrescu. Best of all, he's prolific. Stay up late and read *Night Shift!*"
— Elinor Nauen, author of *American Guys, My Marriage A to Z,* and *So Late into the Night*

"This book is way too short. I would gladly read anything Ron cared to write about: every factory, every bookstore, every bowling alley parking lot. His insights are freakin' hilarious!"
— Sharon Mesmer, author of *Annoying Diabetic Bitch* and *The Virgin Formica*

"Anyone who has ever had a crappy job will read *Night Shift* with bitter affirmation."
— Sparrow, author of *How to Survive the Coming Collapse of Civilization*

For Bud Smith,
with immense gratitude!

NYC.
12/7/18
best!!
R. K

Night Shift

UNBEARABLE BOOKS / AUTONOMEDIA
Series Editors: Jim Feast and Ron Kolm

Night Shift

Stories by Ron Kolm

Unbearable Books/Autonomedia

Front cover photo by Daniel Kolm.
Back cover photo by Arthur Kaye.

Some of these stories appeared in *The Brooklyn Rail, Public Illumination Magazine, The Unbearables, Crimes of the Beats, The Worst Book I Ever Read, The Unbearables Big Book of Sex, Local Knowledge, Flapperhouse, Sensitive Skin, Great Weather for Media,* and the *In Case We Die* anthology (Unknown Press).

Sections of the "The Plastic Factory" were first published in *Appearances* magazine, *Public Illumination Magazine,* the *Saltimbanque Review, Far Out Further Out Out of Sight* and *Redtape.* The entire text appeared in the November, 2011, *Brooklyn Rail.* It was published as a chapbook by Red Dust in 1989 and a revised edition was published by Autonomedia in 2011.

Graphics: Bob Witz, David Sandlin, Dan Freeman, Gregory Kolm, Shalom Neuman, James Romberger, Bill Anthony, Larry Deyab, Ken Brown, Clayton Patterson, Bob Eckstein, Jeffrey Isaac and Fly.

Unbearables: www.unbearables.com

Autonomedia
POB 568 Williamsburgh Station
Brooklyn, NY 11211-0568 USA
info@autonomedia.org
www.autonomedia.org

Table of Contents

"Industrial Sandwich"   Bob Witz

A Philadelphia Story

I worked in a bookstore in Reading, Pennsylvania, when I was in college. It was quite different from a New York City bookstore; we sold furniture, school supplies and an interesting assortment of snacks. I did my best to make the stock we carried respectable; I ordered Joyce, Beckett and Updike, who had lived in Shillington, a suburb of Reading, in his youth. Most of our customers just wanted a fast read. I sympathized, but pushed my favorite authors on them anyway. The owner would take me aside and tell me to cut it out. I'd shrug my shoulders and he'd hiss: "Only bums do that."

I didn't like him very much.

There was a lot of dead time; Reading was not a reading city; so I would flip through the art books and look at the color plates to get through the long afternoons. I discovered the Surrealists, and that's when my life changed. I made up my mind that someday I would be part of a circle of writers and artists just like them. And then, by logical extension, I stumbled upon the Dadaists. Marcel Duchamp became my idol — I devoured his works: "The Bride Stripped Bare," "Nude Descending a Staircase" and "The Chocolate Grinder." I read that a number of his pieces were in the Philadelphia Museum of Art, in the Arensberg Collection, and that his final work, "Given: 1. The Waterfall, 2. The Illuminating Gas," a mixed media assemblage consisting of a wooden door surrounded by bricks concealing something, was there, too. But I couldn't find an illustration or description of what was behind it anywhere, so I knew I would have to go to the City of Brotherly Love and check it out in person.

My parents still lived outside of Philly in the house I'd grown up in. I went down to see them and made plans to visit the Museum.

Unfortunately, when I did manage to get there the wing of the Museum with the Arensberg Collection in it was closed to the public due to budget cuts. A fiscal crisis had swept across the nation, and it hit Philadelphia hard. The Museum of Art is like a large U; basically two wings jutting out from the main building, and they only had enough money to guard one wing at a time. I'd have to return when the side of the Museum I wanted to see was open. Deeply disappointed, I took the commuter train back up to Chestnut Hill and hitched a ride — you could do that back then — to where I was staying with my parents.

On a day I knew the wing of the Museum I wanted to see *should* be open, I headed back into center city. It was raining lightly when I left home, and I took an umbrella figuring that everything would work out okay. I'd take the train in, make my way over to the Benjamin Franklin Park-way; and then walk along the six lane highway a half mile or so to where it ends; at the "Rocky" steps of the Philadelphia Museum of Art. No problem.

But there was a problem. By the time I got into the city, the rain had picked up, and turned into a gale. I could see the Parkway about half a block in front of me, but my umbrella blew inside out, and the rain was now gusting at me in horizontal torrents. I literally couldn't move forward. So I stood in the lee of a large tree, totally deflated. My clothes were soaked, my shoes were covered with mud, and I couldn't imagine how I was going to get home. I'd probably still be there but for a minor miracle.

From out of nowhere, a bus pulled up next to my tree, the doors swooshed open, and the driver waved me inside. I gratefully complied. Once I got in, I exhaled deeply, and examined my surroundings. Every seat on the bus was occupied by an elderly white haired lady.

"We told him to stop and pick you up," a woman sitting in the front explained, giggling a little. "You seemed to be stuck!"

"Man," I said, "I was! I am so grateful. Thank you, all of you!"

"Where were you going?" another Lady asked.

"Well, I was hoping to make it to the Art Museum, but that seems to be out of the question now…"

"No, it's ok," a third chimed in. "Driver, take him to the Museum, please. We have lots of time before we have to return to our residence."

And he did.

He let me off at the rear entrance and I ducked inside. It was still raining, but not as hard. The Museum halls were deserted; the weather had taken its toll. I made my way to the nearest men's room where I chucked my broken umbrella. This particular rest room had one of those old fashioned cloth towel dispensers to dry your hands on: the kind that seem to be an endless loop of clean white material. I simply kept pulling out portions of towel to dry my hair on, my shirt, my pants and my muddy shoes. I guess I felt kind of guilty when I got to the shoes, but no one came in to use the facilities, so I continued until I had used up the entire roll.

After I'd dried out a bit, I exited into the Museum, aiming towards the right wing, which was to my left, and which was, as I had hoped, open. I walked through the Arensberg Collection where Duchamp's paintings and constructs were displayed, checking them out in a cursory fashion as my eyes were focused on the prize. The building was still empty; I passed only one or two guards, and finally reached a dead end. In this room there was a large wooden farm door, though in truth it was more like a castle gate. It was made of thick planks surrounded by a stone archway. When I walked up to it I noticed two tiny holes had been drilled in the middle. I looked through them. And saw the most wonderful sight.

It was a naked female mannequin, her face obscured by the broken bricks framing the scene, reclining in a field of fake grass, holding aloft a tiny gaslight, which was lit. Behind this tableau was a painted landscape depicting a waterfall. It was obviously an appropriation of the Statue of Liberty — Duchamp's cry for real freedom in the land of the not so free. It was not only a tremendous work of art; what he had done was truly funny! I cracked up: laughing out loud.

A guard rounded the corner with a stern look on his face and wondered what was up.

"I've just seen God," I told him, and left the room.

David Sandlin

I Was a Teenage Fascist

I had a problem relating to other kids almost from the very beginning. My mother was lonely and had a creative temperament which she wasn't able to express publicly, so she would play the piano for hours to a captive audience: me. This confused me — I was only five, so I retreated to the dark space under the kitchen table, taking a small portable radio with me. Soul Music became my best friend; The Coasters, The Platters, Smokey Robinson and The Miracles — they were my constant companions. When I disappeared from view my mother realized that something had changed, so she started giving piano lessons to the neighborhood kids; this gave her a new audience, leaving me alone in my cave, licking my wounds.

When I got old enough to read, I devoured the few books my father had laying around the house from his childhood: *Tom Slade on a Transport*, *Pee-Wee Harris in Luck*, and Horatio Alger's *Sink or Swim*. He also had some Reader's Digest Condensed Books that I think he'd rescued from the trash during a Boy Scout paper drive. I'm going to blame Tom Slade for the next turn my young brain took — a drift into fascism — because his spellbinding adventure took place during the Great War. I believe most fascists are tormented teenagers at heart; unable to empathize with other people, angry at their social isolation, wanting to force folks to pay attention to them; and that's why so many of them get into weapons and military stuff.

I got fixated on war and killing for those same reasons. I asked my mom if she would buy me some books on the subject so I could satisfy my curiosity. She was more than happy to; it fit in with her notion of the creative life; I would now turn out to be an artist like her — a writer rather than a pianist, true, but that was ok. But I was heading in a different direction. We went to the mall and the first book I picked out was *Battle: The Story of the Bulge* by John Toland. And it got worse. *Rise and Fall of the Third Reich*, *Stuka Pilot*, *Panzer Leader*, *Mein Kampf* — I read them all. I became a self-loathing non-Jew, sitting in my bedroom, stewing in all the sad juices of my loneliness and despair. I had a plastic luger I would wave around, shooting at the shadows as they converged on me.

I am so lucky that my mom got me a copy of *Catch 22* by mistake, thinking it was a war book like all the others. That book, with its humanity and humor, changed my life. I went on to read the Beats; *Howl*, *Coney Island of the Mind* and *On the Road*; books I bought myself. I was scared; I'd finally come to the realization of just how far from normal human interaction I'd gotten.

When I went away to college I gladly left behind all the labels that had been attached to me in high school: one of those being 'loser.' One night, while hanging out in front of the freshmen dorm with some friends, I flagged down a white MGA sports car and asked the girl who was driving it if she would give me a ride, and she said yes. And even though it was only a ride up Mount Penn and back, no sex, no kissing even, I knew I had entered a new world. I asked her if I could see her again, and she said 'yes' again. I found out later that she wrote poetry, and I asked her what that entailed. She showed me some of her work and I never looked back.

> (This piece was written and performed
> for Phillip Giambri's Losers Club reading
> at the Cornelia Street Café, 1/6/2016.)

Dan Freeman

Maupin Row I

Vietnam was on, and I only barely managed to avoid it by volunteering to work as a community organizer in Appalachia. My wife volunteered too.

We had such big plans for the folks there — we were going to bring them streetlights and sewers — hell, we were even going to try to fix the polluted creek that ran through the middle of Maupin Row, the collection of rickety shacks we lived in. I still had this beautiful vision in the back of my mind as I watched snowflakes drift down between the worn slats of our ancient outhouse and melt on my bare knees.

We smoked dope all winter and listened to Led Zep. When spring finally came, the best we could do was a second-rate clean-up campaign. The town fathers never came through with the dumpster they'd promised, so I had to use my brand-new '69 pick-up truck to haul the garbage away — the wooden bed in the back buckled and splintered under the weight of old tires and broken sofas.

"Too bad about your truck," my wife said.

"It's ok," I said in a shaky voice, trying not to lose it.

Dan Freeman

Maupin Row II

We were totally unprepared for the winter of 1968; it was bleak and cold, and it seemed to last forever. My wife and I were from the North — Reading, Pennsylvania — and we had joined a government program to help organize the dispossessed so they could eventually help themselves. This program was called VISTA, which stands for Volunteers In Service To America. What it really was was my ticket out of Vietnam — if I volunteered to help the poor, then I wouldn't get drafted — it was called 'alternative service.'

The folks we were supposed to be helping were Southerners. Poor Southerner whites. Rednecks. After training in Atlanta, we got sent to Tennessee, to the tri-cities area on the Tennessee/Virginia border — the three cities were Bristol, Kingsport and Johnson City. We ended up in a hollow just outside the Johnson City city limits. The locals had named this particular hollow 'Maupin Row,' and it was a sad collection of dilapidated wooden shanties lining several narrow dirt roads which were clustered around a polluted creek. If you were driving on the city road that circled Maupin Row you couldn't actually see it — you had to turn off the main drag and cut through a sort of high hedgerow — the "community" such as it was, then opened out below you.

We lived in the same type of housing as the people we'd been sent to help — basically a two-room shack with a tiny kitchen hanging off the back. We also had an outhouse. Maupin Row was zoned outside the city limits so it had no sewage system and no garbage pick-up — the people who lived there only got cold running water, and the city was going to keep it that way if they could. Putting in sewers and picking up trash cost money and as the poor weren't able to pay any taxes, they simply weren't worth wasting time on.

Our neighbors were actually very nice to us. Mrs. Jones, who lived with her family on the dirt road that intersected with ours, tried to show us how to bank a coal fire so it would last through the night. The secret was to surround the heart of the fire with enough combustible material to provide fuel for it, but not enough to smother the life out of it. A coal fire banked correctly would smolder slowly, lasting almost until dawn. The only drawbacks were the inevitable fumes, but the shack we lived in was so drafty that that problem was moot.

I never did get the hang of it. Once winter settled in we had to punt; we drove to the local discount store and bought an electric blanket and a large electric heater; we figured that this would be enough to make one room livable; the bedroom. The rest of our tiny home we abandoned to the cold — and it was so cold in the living room that we could put the milk and soda on the floor below the window, where they kept just fine. Meats, and any other frozen goods, were stashed on the windowsill, where they stayed frozen. I guess I should mention that we didn't have a refrigerator — the house didn't come with one, and we didn't have enough money to buy one, so we ate most of our meals in fast food joints.

They got to know us pretty well in the local McDonald's. The bitter cold made sex difficult, almost impossible. Moving around under the electric blanket created a storm of static electricity that snapped and crackled and gave us a continuous series of painful shocks — it was like trying to couple on a bed of hot coals. It we threw the cover off we froze our asses, and if we made it to any kind of climax, the wet cum would almost short the damn thing out. We ended up huddling together under the toasty blanket and watching a lot of late night television — Johnny Carson became our best friend.

We finally came up with an ingenious solution to solve our sexual woes; we'd hop into our half ton pickup truck, drive to the East Tennessee State University parking lot, and fuck in the cab while keeping the engine running and the heater on. We'd usually keep the radio on, too.

Of course this solution had its drawbacks. Because we were never sure if some sort of security would eventually show up and chase us off, we had to work quickly. Foreplay was minimal — a little making out, and that was about it. My wife would then kind of sit on my lap, where I'd hoist her up and down on my trusty dick, gripping her by the hips, groaning in the throes of ecstasy, and she'd end up hitting her head on the window, or on the roof of the truck cab, with each thrust, shouting out more in pain than pleasure.

On good nights, when we weren't fighting and had time to plan ahead, my wife would wear a dress that buttoned up the front and dispense with undergarments altogether. Sometimes she'd really get into it and wear a garter belt and silk stockings; she knew that turned me on. Unfortunately, whenever she wore them they usually got runs and were ruined.

"Shit, Ronnie," she'd say, "I'm gonna have to throw this pair out, too! Take it easy! This fucking truck fucking thing is really pissing me off! Maybe we should just stop having sex 'til spring…"

When it snowed she'd wear high leather boots, and she'd be stomping all over my feet when she did finally get off — the puddles of melted snow on the floor of the truck cab would squish and splash, and splatter the truck's interior in interesting ways.

One time, after we started humping, things devolved into a huge fight. She was pissed off that I hadn't brushed my teeth before we left the house, and the fact that I probably hadn't bathed in a while didn't help; the smell in the truck was pretty ripe. The only time we could take a bath was when we visited with the other VISTA volunteers, which wasn't that often — most of them lived in Kingsport, a long drive in the snow. They had been assigned to help a more urban population; mostly folks who lived in projects. So those volunteers had been placed in regular homes with bathrooms and refrigerators. Whenever we did drive up to Kingsport, it was a real treat to get cleaned up and become almost normal again.

Anyway, after we screamed at each other, she jumped out of the truck half-naked, but with her boots still on, and ran off into the snowy night. I zipped up, and charged out after her. I was slipping and sliding on the ice covered asphalt, but I finally caught up with her and we tumbled down onto the ground together. I picked her up and we made our way back to the warmth of the truck. I was scared; this was something new. Our fights had never gone this far before. I clung to her tightly; she was shaking from the cold, and I turned the dashboard heater up as high as it would go.

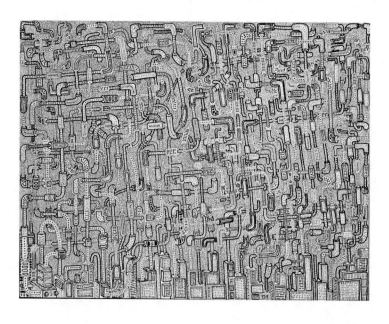

Gregory Kolm

The Plastic Factory

I

My name is Ron, I work in a plastics factory. The particular factory I work in is new, and it squats atop a manmade mound of grass-covered rubble. In front of it is a large asphalt parking lot with an access road tying it to a major highway which, in turn, eventually bypasses a medium sized city. To one side of the factory are miles of flat sparse fields, traveling out to a low range of blue mountains in the distance. The other side drops down to a curve in the expressway.

The factory itself is modern architecture at its most functional and banal; the one-storied rectangular box. Only three appendages break this stark harmony; a loading dock on the left front, the main door on the right front, giving the design balance, and a toolshed in back. Halfway down the steep embankment, between the factory and the highway, is a small square concrete structure. We call it the "pillbox."

The factory's interior is split along its length into two equal halves by a spacious hallway. Access to this hall is controlled by the office, the first cubicle on the right side. The main entrance leads into this office. Continuing down the hall, we pass on our right the locker room, where the employees change into their white smocks, the bathrooms and the dispensary, and finally a modern, well-lit cafeteria, with its plastic chairs and formica'd tables, and its banks of tall bright fast-food machines. If we retrace our steps back to the front of the building, and list the rooms on our left as we repeat our journey towards the rear, we'd first pass an immense space directly behind the loading dock. This is the inspection, packing and shipping room. Beyond this, protected by thick double walls of cinderblock, is the pressure cooking room, the room I work in.

My shift runs from three o'clock in the afternoon to midnight, with an hour break for lunch, which is really dinner. There is only one other person who works this shift with me, and the reason for this is the brand-newness of our plant.

Over fifty people work in this factory during the first shift, which starts at six in the morning and ends at three. First shift sets their alarm clocks for five A.M. They awake in pitch darkness. Second shift, my shift, is being built-up gradually. So far, just the two of us. There is no third shift. The factory is closed between twelve and six.

Most of the employees have what they consider to be decent jobs. They wear clean smocks. They work in a clean, safe area. They're allowed to listen to portable radios. And they get paid fairly well, all things considered equal. But for my partner and me, and for our counterparts on the first shift, conditions are somewhat different.

You see, what the inspectors are inspecting, and the packers are packing, and the shippers shipping, what the people in the office are drawing-up bills and invoices for, what the investors are making money on, are lenses for eye-glasses, but not ordinary glass lenses, no. The lenses we manufacture are made of plastic, using a new and still secret process. This secret is guarded in many and ingenious ways; for instance the entire building, and the pillbox outside, are wired to Wells Fargo, and so on.

But let us discuss the process, itself. A mixture containing styrene, an oil-based fluid, and an excimer, is poured into a form, which is placed in a giant pressure cooker, and baked, or broiled, or what have you. The temperature in our room is almost unbearable at times. The heat acts on the excimer, causing it to change chemically, and when the form is removed from the machine, some eight hours later, the liquid inside it has hardened into a tough, clear sheet of lenses. These lenses are then separated, cleaned, inspected and packed for shipping. But, let me repeat, only two people on the first shift, and my partner and I on the second, work in the bright, hot room containing the pressure cookers.

The wall on one side of our room is thin and corrugated, and is termed a "safety-wall" by the factory's insurance company. This means that if one of the machines explodes, instead of spewing destruction in all directions, possibly into the separating or inspection area, the force, seeking the path of least resistance, will push this wall outward, away from the rest of the building. Only two people need disappear.

The ceiling in our room is supported by a network of bare steel girders, and festooned with fiery bright floodlights. Our room is bathed in artificial brilliance. Every object in our room, the machines, the walls, the girders, ourselves, becomes unreal in the harsh glare. These lights are special helium arc lamps, and when they suddenly flicker and die, which they frequently do because the factory's generator is new and unreliable, our room is plunged into utter hot darkness. Our room has no emergency lighting system, because the styrene mixture we use is flammable. Thus, portable radios, flashlights, matches and anything else that might cause a fire are prohibited in our work area.

That is, the styrene is flammable only until it is poured into the machine. At which point its flammability becomes an asset instead of a liability. Once we've got it inside the machine, it's *supposed* to expand, though admittedly at a slower rate than it would like. This property of styrene, its desire to expand rapidly, makes it a difficult material to handle. You see, it especially wants to rebel at room temperature — to express itself pyrotechnically, so to speak. Because of this unfortunate tendency towards violence, it must be stored in a large refrigerator at one end of our room. Styrene is shipped and stored in huge shiny steel drums. We remove one from the freezer on a hand truck, place it on the prongs of a forklift, and raise the cold drum high into the air. At the bottom of the drum is a petcock and rubber tube affair, which is attached to a filling machine, similar in size and shape to an eight cylinder automotive engine block. The styrene is thus gravity fed into the filling machine.

The filling machine, a massive piece of complications, is mounted on a large chain hoist, so it too can be raised or lowered. However, this process of loading the filling machine has not yet been perfected. We only know it's full when noxious streams of styrene splash to the concrete floor. The overflow can then be stemmed by shutting the petcock and lowering the forklift.

Now this filling machine, suspended on its chain hoist from two long overhead rails, is able to traverse the entire length of the room, enabling it to service all four of the pressure cookers. My partner pushes, while I pull it into position, slipping on the treacherously deceptive puddles of styrene as they play out behind us. The filling machine leaks constantly. Once we've managed to bully it into the proximity of the pressure cooker we're about to use, half of the battle is won. The other half is occupied with coupling twelve tiny translucent tubes between the two bulky inanimate objects, while fierce streams of styrene spray about our persons.

Styrene is possessed of strange properties.

It eats away the rubber soles of our shoes. It gobbles at bare skin. It devours eyeballs.

The barrels of styrene are clearly labeled "Non-Life-Supportive."

Which means an atmosphere of pure styrene would kill you quick. Each time I enter the freezer to remove a drum, I gag on the stench, my head spins, I almost blackout, but if I'm lucky, and fast enough, I know I'll probably emerge intact, it's happened before. I usually survive.

In some ways styrene is poetic ... it has poetic qualities. Styrene is one of the ingredients in model airplane cement. And model airplane cement, ingested through the nostrils, can alter a person's consciousness. More than one Nirvana has been sealed by this method.

And styrene smells.

The smell gets in your clothes, your hair, everywhere. It has a very distinctive smell. People tend to avoid you. You become a pariah, an outcast, an abnormality.

But I digress. The connections are finally made, the forms inside the pressure cooker are filled, the filling machine is dragged away, and the switch turned on.

II.

My wife and I live in a decaying two-hundred year old stone farmhouse, which clings precariously to the side of a steep embankment. It goes from three stories in the front — living room, bedroom, attic — to five stories in the rear — tool shed, kitchen, parlor-bathroom, back bedroom, attic. The size and shape of our house — it's not ours, we rent — presents us with a constant series of problems. For example, if, in the middle of the night, I want a snack, or some juice to take an aspirin with, I must descend from the front bedroom to the living room, and then from the living room to the kitchen, leaving a diagonal trail of turned-on lights behind me.

If, while in the kitchen, I hear a noise in our backyard, on our mountain, I have to exit from the kitchen door onto a crumbling cement walkway, flashlight in one hand, the other groping for the rusted iron railing, and trundle carefully down a tilted flight of badly chipped steps to the slope below. Luckily, or unluckily, the bedroom is so far removed from the kitchen that it's impossible to hear anything out back.

The incline falls away so sharply that when I wander into the back bedroom to look for a book, or a magazine, or just to ponder my fate, and happen to glance, absent-mindedly, out upon the world behind our house, I'm always surprised by how small — how far away everything is. Sometimes the view exhilarates me, if things are going well, but if I'm depressed, which seems to be the case more often than not these days, it adds an even greater distance between me and any peace of mind.

From this vista, following the base of the house downward, the hill, dotted by tall clumps of twisted pine, finally flattens into a stubbly clearing, traversed by a small creek. Beyond the creek is a large field, and beyond the field a highway, which replaced the road our house fronts on. Beyond the highway is a shopping center. The shopping center is flanked by several heavily populated subdivisions. Rising far behind this strip of activity are the same blue mountains that I can see through the steel grates that cover the side windows of the plastics factory.

I live only a couple of miles from where I work.

The interior decoration of the house was bequeathed to us by the previous tenant. The living room walls — two feet thick, that's how they built them years ago, and all solid stone — are wallpapered in a zig-zag pattern of random reds, oranges and greens. It had to take a deranged sensibility to design such a mess ... but why did the single woman with her two children who lived here before us select it for her home? God knows, she must have seen some strange corners of truth while sitting in that room watching TV.

The windows, however, are nice, as the thickness of the walls gives way to recessed sills, deep enough to sit on comfortably. The thinner walls of the parlor-bathroom, a later addition to the basic house, are papered in a silvery confection, so clearly reflective, that one can watch one's self on the toilet.

The front and rear bedrooms were a shambles when we moved in, the wallpaper flaking and peeling in long discolored strips. I scraped through layers of ancient paper and paint, finally exposing the pockmarked plaster base. I sealed and painted the walls of the two rooms as best I could — but whenever it rains portions give way and crumble to the floor in small mounds of gaudy dust.

The attic is beyond help. The roof, an old slate and wood beam type, leaks like a sieve — and the landlord says that the only way to fix it is to put on a whole new set of slates, which he can't afford to do, do we want to move? But, as the rent is dirt cheap, a hundred-and-twenty-five a month for an entire house, we say no, and stay on.

I've constructed a series of metal troughs, running them from the worst of the leaks to the eaves, where I cut a number of openings for drainage. It actually seems to work to some degree, and though the plaster walls beneath still continue to disintegrate, at least there isn't any more flooding in the bathroom or kitchen.

Just describing the physical condition of my surroundings is tiring ... but I've been avoiding the central issue ... and that is that I'm going through a terrible period in my life. My marriage isn't working out.

My wife and I have become enemies, of a sort. She can't stand the smell of plastic I drag around with me like a shroud. The house stinks of it — my work shoes, soaked with caustic styrene, sit in the furnace room decaying into their cardboard and leather components. Inerasable black footprints have stained the kitchen floor forever. The kitchen door is the only one I'm allowed to use when returning from work. I stumble into the dark chilly kitchen after midnight, gagging on my own stench, tear off my deformed boots, throw them in the general direction of the basement, open a beer, and try to drink myself back to sanity. Quite often I settle for gentle oblivion. Sometimes the smell is so strong in my hair, even after washing it, that I'm forced to make my bed on the living room couch, and I lie there, nursing a beer, looking at the nutty wallpaper, and think about my wife sleeping directly above me.

My wife, to save her life I suppose, has created a new lifestyle right before my eyes. She's hung beaded curtains between the doorways, and cluttered the house with broken antique furniture. Vintage movie posters stare back at me from the walls. Strange electrical appliances proliferate — juicers and blenders and can openers and hairdryers and waterpiks and humidifiers and crock pots and so on. She works in a health food store, and takes handfuls of vitamins all the time — her purse is filled with them. Also, she's joined a spa, and I'm sure she's having an affair with her physical therapist. I'm bitter, I'm bitter, and worse, this problem is all my fault.

I'm going through a nervous breakdown. No, that's not entirely true. I'm going through a breakdown of the imagination. That is true. I have no conception of the future any more, and having no conception of the future means that I'm stuck here in an everlasting present, passively letting events flow over me like waves on the beach. I can't seem to think my way out of the dilemmas I'm faced with ... if it was one problem, or two, I might have a chance, but the job, the house, and my relationship are all tied together — and on top of everything the Arab nations have placed an oil embargo on my country. What this means in practical terms is that on a Saturday, let's say, I'm supposed to meet my wife in the city at her place of work for dinner, or a movie, if we should happen to have the extra money — but I sit in my car, in a line of cars, in a long line of very slowly moving cars, looking at my watch, feeling my stomach twist into knots, knowing that by the time I finally get two dollars of gas, because that's all they'll give, and drive into town, whatever good time we might have had will be irretrievably lost. She'll be furious.

Where were you, why are you late, why didn't you plan ahead, have you been drinking? And she's right, I seem to trap myself, plan my own destruction. My wife is so much quicker than me, especially in the emotional sphere. She seems to have identified my impasse and is bailing out. While I tread water. Drinking too much. And returning day after day to a plastics factory.

IIIA.

The pillbox is a six-foot cube of concrete, surrounded by barbed-wire, housing two massive freezers. Each of these freezers has its own thermostat, and each thermostat is wired to the local Wells Fargo Protective Agency. If either thermostat begins to register a rise in temperature an alarm is automatically triggered, causing a Wells Fargo employee to telephone the plant with the bad news. The reason for such an elaborate warning system is this: the freezers are used to store the excimer, which creates the chemical reaction during the pressure cooking process, before it's mixed into each batch of styrene. And if styrene is highly flammable, the excimer alone is downright explosive. At room temperature styrene will evaporate if not constricted; the excimer will detonate violently. However, once the frozen excimer is dropped into a barrel of styrene it dissolves, becoming much more docile, ready to perform its task. If a freezer-fail is not corrected, the pillbox and its contents would be demolished in a bright flash of sound.

Theoretically, upon receipt of such an emergency call, I must race out of the factory to the pillbox, produce a key, open the barbed-wire gate, and seek an explanation for the malfunction.

If I am unable to coax the freezer back to life with sweet reason or swift kicks, I'm supposed to speed back to the plant, locate the portable generator, which is mounted on two skids like a child's sled, drag it down to the concrete enclosure, hook it up to the wounded freezer, and start it with a lawnmower whipcord. When the factory foreman tried to demonstrate this procedure during my training period, he couldn't get the generator going. I asked him what I should do if, just for the sake of argument, the same problem occurred during a real crisis.

"If all else don't work," he answered, "And you're out of gas or whatever, you gotta take the little buggers — the excimer is packed in small clear trays like cuts of meat in a supermarket — and throw them down towards the expressway, so the little buggers will blow-up away from the plant."

Sure — I can just see myself standing on the side of the hill like some kind of crazy person pitching little meat-trays like baseballs, risking my life for three bucks an hour, while frightened drivers swerve about below, stunned by the orange puffs of smoke and concussion. Sure — I'm a sucker — I'd probably do it.

IIIB.

When the hardened sheets of plastic lenses have sufficiently cooled — they're not really cool; in fact, they're usually still hot to the touch, like toast from a toaster — they're removed from the steaming pressure cookers and stacked on specially designed carts.

This act of removing the plastic sheets from the pressure cookers creates a static charge; anytime two materials come into contact and are separated, one assumes a positive charge and the other a negative. The sheets therefore attract copious amounts of dust and lint, like iron filings to a magnet, making them unusable.

The static charge is neutralized by gently waving a two foot long radioactive bar back and forth above each sheet. This bar is the anti-static rod. Its radioactive core — the anti-static rod is registered with the Atomic Energy Commission — to tamper with it, or to remove it from the factory, is to commit a felony — is ionized, which means it contains extra electrons; electrons looking for a more stable environment. And the electron starved plastic sheets provide it. Making everyone happy. The electrons, the lenses, the factory owners; everyone, that is, except me. While doing its job, the rod, I fear, is also doing something else, something not so nice.

Every time I wave this magic wand over the sheets of plastic like some kind of demented tooth fairy, my white smock billowing around me with the motion, my gut tightens, my sperm die. I'm sure of it. My wife and I don't talk about it, but working here is probably making me sterile. And possibly, at the same time, mutating my cells, opening the genetic door to cancer, that unwelcome though everpresent guest.

IV.

No particular violence. A winter sun is high above the house, far away. I hustle out of bed and into my clothes, shivering in the cold, and stumble down two flights of stairs to the kitchen. My wife is long gone. To her job at the health food store. Or where-ever. She didn't move when I eased myself into bed after work last night, though I doubt she was asleep. She's turned into quite a good little actress lately, despite the limitations of her role.

Opening a beer, I survey our poverty pocket of a re-frigerator. A few lonely leftovers working their way back to nature, sitting unwrapped on tiny chipped saucers. Butter. Brussel sprouts. Meatballs. Also, a half-finished carton of milk. And a small project of Tupperware con-tainers filled with various unlabeled grains and powders. But I'm not about to mess with the unknown. Give me a Big Mac any day.

So I sip at my beer and stare out the kitchen window. And curse my wife because she's got the family car, which is really a truck, which means I'm stuck here until I have to leave for work. My wife and I share a GMC pick-up truck. It's pure white, with a bright red interior. We used to take turns driving it, but the overlap in our jobs — she works days, I work nights — killed that arrangement. Now she uses it almost exclusively. And I bum rides to work with my partner.

My partner's name is Arnold Sebniewski. He's a short fellow with long black hair slicked back in a glossy high-rolling pompadour. He married a young girl, a very young girl. A child-bride of sixteen. And they play house in a poor neighborhood.

Bad luck continually nips at his heels, never quite devouring him whole. His car is an antique gas-guzzler. A living fossil he can't afford. But he's in a bind. No one would buy it if he tried to sell, and he needs a means to get to work. So every day I stand on the side of the highway praying for the well-being of his junk heap, and breathe a sigh of relief when it finally heaves into view.

Arnie chain smokes. And this habit, since you're not allowed to smoke in our work space, makes him manic at work. He runs in and out of the pressure cooking area all night long like a terminally nervous whirling dervish, his smock covered with ashes and cigarette burns.

And he can't see too well either. Arnold wears thick glasses that keep falling off his head to the greasy concrete floor. He picks them up and wipes them on his dirty smock, grinding oily crud into the lenses. He's effectively blind. Combine this handicap with his nicotine craving and the result is an interesting series of problems.

For example: The forklift we use in our room to shuffle around the barrels of styrene is an electrically-controlled hand-operated affair. It's large and powerful. A useful machine. Arnie was fooling with it one night, and he managed to simultaneously start it and lock it into reverse. The forklift playfully backed him into a wall and, the handle jammed in his gut, raised him six inches from the floor. I thought he would be gored to death, while I stood there watching helplessly, a knot of fascinated fear expanding inside me.

But the machine's safety switch shut off, leaving him suspended in the air, very much alive, his tiny feet kicking about.

Another time, bored by the routine of our job, he climbed up on one of the hissing pressure cookers, reached for an exposed girder high above him, and pulled himself on top of it. He stood up slowly, a bit shaky, and grinned down at me. He then did a little victory dance to celebrate his feat, lost his footing, and fell to the floor. I couldn't believe it. I rushed over to his twisted body, expecting to find his back broken, or his neck snapped, but once again bad luck had merely tapped him on the shoulder and then departed for a while. His smock was soaked with dark patches of styrene, his hair was matted with the stuff, his eyes were closed, but he seemed intact.

I carefully lifted him from the floor, filled with a mixture of pity and disgust, and carried him to the infirmary, where I rinsed his eyes with warm water. Leaving him there, bathed in the eerie green infirmary light, I returned to our room to check the temperature levels. I didn't want the whole factory to blow up. At least not while we were in it.

Seconds later he reappeared in the room, looking no worse for the wear, an unlit cigarette dangling from the corner of his mouth.

V

The pressure cookers are essentially huge hot water heaters, with built-in thermostats and timers. With their lids shut they look like large rectangular stainless-steel coffins. Inside each pressure cooker are thirteen movable cast-iron plates and a hydraulic arm that projects towards them from the right inner wall. Assembled forms are placed between the plates, and then the entire sandwich — plate, form, plate, form — is compressed by activating the hydraulic arm, making it airtight. This keeps the styrene inside the forms and the boiling water out. The forms are filled, tiny plugs hammered into the pour holes with a rubber mallet, the water intake valve turned on, and the machine is ready to run.

The forms into which we pour the styrene are also sandwiches. The core of each form is a three-quarter inch thick steel pattern with twenty-four convex glass inserts. An aluminum "cupcake tray" with twenty-four matching concave impressions is placed on either side of the core. Both aluminum end pieces are edged with compressible rubber gaskets. The three pieces that make up a finished form are held together with metal clamps, the same kind high-school students use to bind their term papers.

After the forms have been locked into place inside the pressure-cookers, the clamps are knocked off with a hammer and screwdriver.

The gaskets are a bitch to put on. They're made of tough white rubber that doesn't bend easily. We cut them in twelve foot lengths from a big spool, and throw them on a hot pressure cooker, making them more pliable, until we're ready to use them. As you begin to edge an aluminum "cupcake tray" with the warm rubber your hands blister, but by the time you reach the final razor-cut the material is cold and intractable. And the gaskets have to be cut precisely — a mistake can ruin an entire run of twenty-four lenses. I've seen my partner murder a gasket with a ball-peen hammer, hitting it again and again on the floor.

After each run is completed, the forms are taken apart, the hard sheets of lenses removed, the melted gaskets pried off and thrown away, the cores vacuumed carefully, and the aluminum "cupcake trays" banged back into shape. There is often a lot of crystalline dark-brown plastic waste stuck to the various parts of the pressure cookers, styrene that has oozed out of minute leaks and partially vaporized, partially burned. This plastic waste has to be chipped from the metal surfaces and swept up. My partner handles the cleaning chores while I wheel the lenses to the packing and inspection area.

We construct extra forms during the period of time it takes the pressure cookers to complete their runs. We're always far ahead of the machines. The owners of the plant are continually devising new ways to collapse the time it takes to bake a batch of lenses, but we still end up with a lot of time on our hands, and the owners are not around to supervise us during the bulk of our shift. We have different ways of making the long nights at work go a little faster — my partner takes drugs and I drink.

He gets his stuff from two of his friends, both Vietnam Vets who survived the war — one was a tank commander and the other a marine. The marine stepped on a buried artillery shell one day while walking point for his squad. A booby-trap. He should have disappeared, a small pink mist dissipating over a muddy trail far away from any plastics factory. But the detonator was defective. The explosion occurred anyway, trapped inside his brain, where it goes off periodically, and the only way he knows how to defuse it is with strong medicine — speed, acid, quaaludes.

They sneak up to the cafeteria window, commando-style, jimmy it open with a large hunting knife, and ease their way into the factory — this is the only way to bypass the Wells Fargo security system that protects the plant. We sit at a formica table in the empty cafeteria, darkness pressing against the windows, and do a variety of drugs and alcohol, mixing them with candy bars and cans of soda from the vending machines.

It's usually at this point that I head for the pay phone in the hall to call my wife. I dial her number at the health food store, tell her it's me, and then hang up the receiver so she can call me back. I can only afford the initial dime it takes to reach her.

I don't know why I call her every night. We always end up arguing, but it's a ritual I adhere to faithfully. I open the conversation by asking her how she's feeling, how are things going at work, is her manager still making passes at her. And this kicks it off. I wouldn't know that her manager makes passes at her if she hadn't told me. To be told something like that and not be able to do anything about it — she likes the job, we need the money, so I can't interfere — ties my stomach into knots. Maybe she likes the attention. I pop open a beer and wait for her response.

Are you drinking on the job again, is that why you're so hostile, you don't trust me, we should get a divorce. I apologize and try to change the subject. Sometimes I'm successful on the first attempt. If I'm not, we circle around the topic of trust for a while, until it's clear to both of us that we're just repeating the same old endless, unresolvable argument. Then we move on to a discussion of our finances. How are we ever going to pay next month's rent, the truck payments, fuel bills, etc.

Somehow or other a tenuous peace is finally achieved, and we're able to end the conversation only vaguely dissatisfied. There've been times I've hung up on her in a blind fury, and there've also been times when she broke off the connection abruptly. Like a child picking at a scab on a wound we worry our relationship, but continue on.

I hang up the phone and wander back into the pressure cooking room to check the gauges. I look at the pile of finished forms stacked on the floor, waiting their turn to be filled with styrene. The helium arc lamps are burning brightly, without a flicker. Everything in the room is normal.

I walk through the double set of doors to the inspection and packing area, past the auto-clave where the lenses are washed, over to one of the side windows. Peering through a heavy steel grate I can barely see the outline of the mountains in the distance, darker than the night.

Shalom Neuman

1975

It's starting to snow. Nothing is sticking to the highway, but tiny wind-driven drifts scatter back and forth in front of the pickup truck as I drive to work. A winter storm has been predicted all day, but it hadn't started yet when I pulled out of the driveway. I probably should have called in sick. I hate the damn job — night-shift on an assembly-line — which seems to be killing me in some way or another, but I need the money so I keep showing up and punching in, waiting for something to happen, an accident, anything — looking for a sign that I should quit and move on, but not finding any.

The snow gives me just the excuse I need to go back home; it will probably be a blizzard for sure, and I don't want to get snowed in at the plant — the idea of living on candy bars and Cokes from the vending machines until we get rescued isn't a turn-on — I'm having enough problems with my marriage as it is, and that would only make matters worse, so I turn left off the bypass onto a side road where I can do a U-turn and return to the rundown farmhouse my wife and I live in.

The secondary road I'm now on is very steep, dropping away from the bypass at an extreme angle, and it's much higher in the middle than on the shoulders. After I turn around and start driving back up towards the highway, my truck shifts to the right, sliding on the fresh snow, until it slams into the curb. Nothing I do can budge it. I try the old trick of shifting into third gear and then slowly giving it some gas, but that doesn't work — I guess the grade is just too much for my old pickup truck with its under-powered six cylinder engine.

I turn off the car radio and switch off the ignition, and sit there, considering my options. The only one I can come up with is to leave my truck and walk up to the roadside and try to flag down a passing driver and hitch a ride home, but there were almost no cars on the highway when I turned off it. A kind of pall descends over me, a sort of numbness. I live more than a couple of miles away, too far to walk in the worsening storm, so I sit there, in a complete stasis, watching the falling snow coat the windshield. And then I hear a shout.

I look out the window, then roll it down, white flakes landing on my left knee. Idling beside me is a very peculiar vehicle — a pure white World War II vintage jeep with the words 'Borough of Mt. Penn' stenciled in black letters on its side. The guy sitting in the passenger seat asks me if I need help and when I say, "yeah," he takes a couple of handfuls of rock salt from a bag that seems to be on his lap and tosses them out of his open window in such a way that they land under the wheels of my truck. I know how strange this sounds, but I swear that this is what I see. I turn the key and my pickup comes back to life. I steer the front wheels slightly to the left, gently pumping the gas pedal, and it moves forward, almost as if by magic. The guys in the jeep wave at me as they speed off, and I drive up to the top of the hill and turn right, heading home, as the snow continues to fall.

***

I park the truck in the driveway, walk through a couple of inches of the white stuff, and go into the house. The cat, at least, seems happy to see me back — he probably figures there's food in his immediate future. I unlace my wet work shoes and toss them down the steep stairway that leads to the kitchen, scaring the cat — I'll open a can of tuna for him later.

I sink back into our beat-up sofa in the living-room, and exhale deeply, relieved to finally be home. I still can't wrap my head around what happened out there — it was like some kind of minor miracle — the image of the guy throwing rock salt under my tires is still so vivid — even though it was snowing heavily when it happened, it was like some kind of strange midday sun was shining down on everything, erasing the storm; it all seems so bright in retrospect.

Like the good husband I'm still trying to be, I know I should call my wife at her shitty part-time job at the health food store, and tell her I've bailed out on going to work. I pick up the phone, look for the store number on a piece of paper scotch-taped to it, and dial.

Her manager answers, and, gritting my teeth, I ask if I can speak to my wife. I know the guy is hitting on her, because she's made a point of telling me. Just another reason to love my life. He puts me on hold. I wait a while, and she finally picks up.

"What do you want, Ronnie? You know I'm at work, and they don't like it when I get personal calls."

"Well, it's snowing pretty hard now, so I turned around and came back home…didn't want to get stuck in the plant overnight. They said it might be seven or eight inches…"

"Big deal! I'm gonna stay and finish my shift. Besides, you know I'm going to a party after work — you're just trying to mess up my evening!"

"No, really," I say, trying to defuse the bomb in the room. "It might get pretty bad — I can pick you up after work…"

"My cousin is giving me a ride, you know that. Really, Ronnie, I have to get back to work. Good-bye."

"Okay…bye," I say, putting the phone back on the receiver. I look at the cat who's looking at me. "Jeez," I say to him, "I am so fucked…"

I put a record on the turntable — Jimi Hendrix — and lean back against the cushions. I really have no idea what to do with myself. At least fighting with my wife wasn't boring, but I sure am bored now.

I look out the window at the falling snow, but my mind stays blank. And then it hits me — I know what I can do to get through the rest of the day — I'll do some drugs — always a great way to collapse time. I have a stash of stuff our friends have given us over the years; stuff we haven't gotten around to using, or stuff we're still kind of afraid to try. There's even some stuff in the small box that's a total mystery — I have a friend in California who sends me pills in every letter he mails me — I have no idea what they are, or what they do. I head to the closet and reach behind a stack of sweaters and pull out the stash box. Then go back to the sofa with it to check everything out.

The box has some weed in it; I know what that is, and some mushrooms. My wife has pretty much stopped doing drugs, and I only smoke marijuana when I listen to music before hitting the sack. But I want something stronger; not a lot stronger, but something to put me in a different space, a better one. Everything looks different than I remember. I check out the pills. I'm pretty sure some of them might be acid, which I still haven't done, but one of them is supposed to be mescaline, which I have done, and which took me on a pretty nice trip. So I opt for the mescaline, and swallow the rather tiny black pill. Without water. Then get back to Hendrix.

But I've made a mistake; the pill I've taken is not mescaline — it turns out to be acid, or so I guess as my world goes somewhere else. I see hideous angels outside the windows, banging on the glass, trying to get in. Everything is moving and breathing.

I watch my cat tearing back and forth across the room; he must know something is awry. I want to play with him; heck, I want to *be* like him — I want to express my inner cat — so I get down on all fours and start prowling around on the floor beside him, which really spooks him out. He starts clawing at the plants we have on either side of the couch. I tear at them, too. We really fuck with them. Somewhere in the back of my mind I know my wife isn't going to like this adventure I'm having very much. Then the cat goes over to his kitty litter and pees and then covers the piss. I don't have to pee, but I run my fingers through the gray gravel as if I had. The cat is absolutely wide-eyed in disbelief.

My personality begins to peel away as if I'm an onion; layer after layer. Memories flash by, and then disappear. When I get to what seems to be the very core of my being I freak out; there isn't anything there I recognize. I simply can't handle what I'm going through. I try calling friends to ask for help, but no one's home. Or perhaps I'm using the phone wrong. I finally manage to call the health food store again, and eventually my wife gets on the phone:

"Ronnie, what the hell do you want? Why are you doing this to me? I have to get off the phone — right now!"

"But, honey, I think I just dropped some acid...something like that...I'm really fucked up..."

"I don't care! You're just doing this to piss me off!"

"Please, dear, please let me pick you up. I'll take you anywhere you want to go. I think I need help..."

"Okay, I'll leave work and start walking along the by-pass. It's probably still snowing. This really sucks, Ronnie!"

She hangs up the phone, and then I do too, looking at it for a long while. Maybe it's only a couple of minutes, though it seems like hours — then I get a pair of slippers from the closet and put my coat on, and head out the front door to my truck. I'm still quite high, but things have lev-elled off to a degree where I can sort of function, but mostly in a reactive way. It's like I'm outside of myself watching me go through the motions.

It's now evening, and the snow has stopped falling — there's almost a foot of it, and my slippers are soaked by the time I get into the truck. I turn on the engine and back out of the driveway, glad I have a pick-up and not a regular car. Our road hasn't been plowed yet, but my vehicle handles it just fine. I figure I'll head down the hill and drive through the center of Reading and then get on the bypass on the other side of town.

When I hit the city limits I see the most incredible things: cars that have crashed into each other, cars that skidded into snowbanks, cars up on the sidewalks, people yelling at each other. All the stoplights in my direction are blinking yellow, and I seem to be gliding by everything without affect. I don't have to stop once. It's as if I'm watching a film, and everything is one long travelling shot; no edits, no problems. I am there and not there; I am driving, but I'm also the passenger. Other than observing the scenery as it rolls past, I only have one idea in mind: I have to find my wife.

I merge onto the bypass. It's very dark, and the roads are slippery, but there is no other traffic. My headlights illuminate the road in front of me, and a little bit of the shoulder. And then I see her, framed in the light, struggling through the snowdrifts on the side of the highway.

I am amazed at my good luck, but I also sort of take it for granted, too. It is all part of the magic that started so much earlier in the day when I decided not to go to work. The fact that we're out in the middle of nowhere doesn't even enter into my thinking.

I stop and pop open the door on the passenger side and, grinning, tell her to hop in — in my movie this is where the lovers are about to be reunited — but not in hers…

"You fucking asshole, Ronnie! What is wrong with you?"

And I can't wipe the smile off my stupid face. It has become a rictus. I'm the Joker, powerless to change my expression. I want to cry, to shout; yet I sit there frozen, helplessly grinning.

"Take me to the bowling alley at the shopping center, and then go home. I told my cousin to meet me there. What's wrong with you anyway?"

"Um, I took some acid by mistake...I was bored..."

"You really are an idiot! Well, I guess you can still drive — get me to the bowling alley — you know where it is."

Which I do, somehow. When we get there we both get out of the truck and stand behind it to say our goodbyes. The white back-up lights are on; I must have parked in reverse; the engine is idling and exhaust is trailing up from the tail pipe, which is vibrating slightly. All of my powers of concentration are focused on that one point — condensation is dripping out the end of it and splattering, ever so slightly, on bare asphalt; most of the parking lot had been plowed before we got there; high mounds of snow surround us.

I keep looking down, lost, and my wife finally says, "Okay, let's go home — I'll drive." And our relationship continues on a little while longer.

"Butler Stacks"   James Romberger

The Worst Book I Ever Read

The worst book I ever read was one I wrote myself. I'm not trying to be cute, or ironic or anything, and I'm not just talking about lousy prose or a lack of comprehensible plot — though my book had no real plot (at the time I thought 'plot' in a piece of writing was an ethically challenged writer's way of joining the great capitalist plot to keep the people down — you know, like throwing already digested gruel on the ground in front of domesticated animals — I figured a great book should make the reader *work,* thus heightening his, or her, consciousness.) There were no real characters in my manuscript and the prose was pretty crappy, a hodge-podge of Joycean nonsense — most postmodern, read; contemporary, attempts at edgy or avant-garde literature come to grief on the reef of James Joyce.

I recently finished *A Reader's Manifesto: An Attack on the Growing Pretentiousness in American Literary Prose* by B. R. Myers, a screed attacking the second-rate writing of Paul Auster, Cormac McCarthy, Don DeLillo and Annie Proulx, among others. One of Myers' criticisms of their novels is that they suffer from the 'andsies' — sentences that go on forever, subordinate clauses linked to each other by the word 'and.' And, of course, it all goes back to Molly Bloom's soliloquy — one of the more famous passages in twentieth-century writing — and one of the few totally enjoyable and easily understood passages in *Ulysses*. My book suffered from the 'andsies,' too, as well as a plethora of portmanteau words, also invented by Mr. Joyce. And my book was pretentious in other ways, as well. I was a college graduate, full of myself, thinking I knew more about many things than I did. I was so proud of my fucking insights — when I split up with my now ex-wife, one of her best zingers was, "You know what, Ronnie? Every one of your stupid insights was totally wrong!" I was driving a pick-up truck at the time, trying to merge into traffic on a bypass around the city of Reading, Pennsylvania, and I just about wiped out on a guard rail when she said that. Unfortunately, she was right — more about that relationship later.

One of the 'insights' I thought I'd stumbled upon back then was the 'Great Voyage Out and Back' paradigm — the Homeric adventure, then return home, sadder but wiser. Hell, Celine used the same template in *Death on the Installment Plan*. I love the ending of that book when the kid finally makes it home after surviving one horrific event after another, and falls asleep exhausted, his uncle covering him with a coat. So I was determined that my main character, viz; myself, would also undertake a heroic journey, experience sexual awakening and drug-fueled enlightenment in an outsized New York City and finally come full circle to some sort of self-realization back where he (I) started — working in a bookstore. Now this journey had to have a physical dimension as well as a metaphorical one; it had to take place on some sort of map; and as my everyday method of conveyance in the city was the subway, I got me a subway map and drew some coordinates on it that seemed vaguely heroic. The main character, me again, would travel out to a wild party in Brooklyn (Flatbush, if I remember correctly), make a pass at a woman he worked with, get drunk out of his mind, stagger back to the station, get on a Lexington Avenue Express, pass out on the train, awaken in the Bronx car yards in the middle of the night, head back to Manhattan, get breakfast at Veselka, a Ukrainian coffee shop, then make it to work on time — hungover but no worse for the wear.

To make the pilgrimage more Dantesque, I created a gigantic transit conductor to act as tour guide, and I made him sort of evil. I guess on some level he was supposed to be the Devil and the subway was supposed to be kind of a railway to Hell. Truthfully, this wasn't the worst conceit I'd ever come up with — those old subway cars threw up showers of sparks whenever the contacts skipped along the third rail, which was pitted and old, and the lights in those cars were so dicey — those same gaps in the third rail caused numerous momentary blackouts with a strobe-light effect — it was like riding in a rocking, beat-up disco — a rocking, beat-up, fucking *graffitied* disco. Don't forget, this was the era of Taki 182, pre-Keith Haring. Every surface area in every car was tagged — tags over tags — the windows, too.

I remember how I had this conductor, as large as Goya's Colossus, shout over the intercom to watch the closing doors, while slamming them shut instantaneously on unwary passengers entering or leaving the train, almost chopping them in two. Sometimes I had him skip stations with no announcement, other times stop with the train only half in, so passengers exiting would tumble onto the tracks.

"Watch the closing doors!" he'd scream, snapping the doors back and forth, then: "...and have a nice day!"

I coupled this notion with an even sillier one; the subway system as intestines. I mean, on a map they *look* like intestines — and the trains, running through them with a sort of peristaltic motion, reminded me of giant turds humping their way to the anus — which is a sort of terminal. Remember, I was going through a bad time — that's my only excuse for this nonsense. Anyway, once you start talking about turds at play, particularly *Homeric* turds in motion, you end up, inevitably, mentioning, or at least *alluding* to, Ben Jonson's "On the Famous Voyage," a long poem in which two wits row up the Fleet Street Ditch, an open sewer, commenting on all the shitting going on as they pass by. Actually, this piece of writing influenced my book greatly, as I saw parallels between it and the *Odyssey,* and *Ulysses,* as well. Toss in some Jonathan Swift, and a jigger full of sad Sam Beckett, and you pretty much have the ingredients of the stew I was simmering.

Speaking of shit, I did do a bunch of research on the subject for my novel. I built a small library of books on human offal: *The Smallest Room* by Pudney, *Clean and Decent* by Lawrence Wright, *Cleanliness and Godliness — or The Further Metamorphosis — A Discussion of the Problems of Sanitation raised by Sir John Harington, together with Reflections upon Further Progress recorded since that Excellent Knight, by his Invention of the Metamorphosed Ajax, Father of Conveniences, revolutionised the System of Sanitation in this country etc*. by Reginald Reynolds ('jakes,' the British slang for outhouse, comes from Ajax). I also bought the Bantam paperback containing the MIT study for building better toilets — it had diagrams of the splash patterns one created when pissing into old-fashioned urinals, and explained what could be done, design-wise, to keep those droplets off your shoes in the future. I also picked-up a tiny cloth-bound gift book on Thomas Crapper, the Englishman who gave his name to our daily dumps. I should point out that these books were, and are, far from being the worst books in anyone's estimation — many of them are worth a pretty penny today. But this detour into shit has just been another way of avoiding the crux of this matter — the real reason why my book was so bad. My manuscript was evil not so much for what it was, as for what it *did* — broke up my first marriage — flushed it right down the crapper.

The bookstore I was working in at the time was the Strand; a huge un-air-conditioned warehouse full of dusty old used books. Over the course of a year almost every book ever written turned up there. Widows sold them the libraries of their dead husbands, reviewers brought them their unread review copies, and junkies schlepped in with torn shopping bags full of stolen books ripped off from Lower East Side tenements. The owner and his son bought 'em all. And they all had to be priced and shelved. I was one of the shelvers. This meant that I was one of the first employees allowed to go through the individual tomes looking for artifacts and minutiae — letters, interesting bookmarks, ticket stubs, photographs, etc. I crammed all these found objects into my pockets and used them in my manuscript when I got home, treating the material both as building blocks and kismetic guides — I still have scrapbooks filled with this stuff.

I also wrote copious notes for my book throughout the day; scribbled sentences on torn scraps of paper; inked messages on the palms of my hands. By this time, mid-'72, my wife and I were living in New Jersey — exit ten on the turnpike. The commute back and forth to my lousy little bookstore job was daunting. It took an hour and a half each way — that's three hours of death subtracted daily from what was something less than the ideal life. Going to work wasn't so bad, though it was way too early in the morning. Getting home was another story. To catch the 7:05 Suburban Transit bus to Edison I'd have to dash out of the store at closing time, 6:30 on the dot, jog up to the Union Square subway station, grab an 'R' or an 'N' train, walk through the cars from the last to the first to save some time, pushing through the rush hour crush, get out at 42nd Street, then run through the twisting maze of underground passageways that led to the Port Authority Bus Terminal on 8th Avenue. By the time I clambered onto the bus I was a sweaty nervous wreck. I'd sit there drenched, in my dirty t-shirt and jeans, among the well-dressed business commuters like a cancer cell among the healthy. Hell, because I was always the last person to get on, I'd almost always end-up on the engine-hump seat in the rear — the hottest, most cramped spot on the bus. I would sit there writing furiously, in a vain attempt to make my life meaningful, transcribing the notes I'd made earlier at work, turning them into something usable.

The third part of this literary trifecta — first part; collecting material at work, second; organizing it on the bus ride home — began when I got back to the sleazy sub-division we called home: this was the typing part, trying to come up with a couple of pages, even a couple of paragraphs, of serviceable prose. The bus stop where I got off was at a strip-mall parking lot near the two-storied box that contained our apartment. The mall had a Seven-Eleven, where I'd pick up milk and soda and Nabisco peanut-crème patties, my favorite snack. I was gaining a lot of weight eating this junk, but things were so fucked up in other ways that this was only a minor irritant to my wife. When I got in the door she would have the tv on, and she'd usually be making cheese and macaroni for dinner. We'd eat while silently watching sit-coms — we had nothing much to say to each other — by this time she was fixated on a Bob Dylan look-alike she worked with. I figured this was normal enough. My parents didn't seem all that happy, but they were still together, so I assumed this was the way relationships were meant to be.

After dinner I'd sit down at the ancient blue portable typewriter that had gotten me through college. It was mostly plastic, with no heft, but I could bang the shit out of it. I used corrasable paper and, as I was constantly rewriting as I went along, my tiny, much-abused typer was filling with eraser shavings. While I whaled away on my book, my wife would continue to watch tv up through Johnny Carson, then brush her teeth and prepare for bed.

"Ronnie, it's time to go to bed," she'd say.

"Ok," I'd say, "Just give me another minute. I got something going here."

And let's say I did have something going. For instance, there was one part of the subway trip when I wake-up in the Bronx train yard on a layover, drunk out of my mind, that got me off when I was writing it. I had this scene where rusted-out redbirds were being broken up for scrap — something I'd actually seen a couple of years earlier. Crews of maintenance guys with blow torches were cutting large swathes of the cars apart and I swear they were throwing the pieces into the river. At least I think that's what they were doing. In my book this diabolical set-piece was presided over by the monstrous conductor.

"Ronnie, this is your last chance. You're really starting to piss me off!"

"Ok, ok," I'd say. But one page would turn into two, if I was lucky, and maybe even three. Writing for me was so difficult then (it's impossible now) that I couldn't tear myself away from the typewriter. But each page pushed me further away from my wife. They were incremental distances, but they added up — each thickness of paper combining until miles of pulp separated us. There really was only one possible ending to all this, and, of course, that's what happened; we separated and eventually divorced, leaving my book triumphant on the field of battle — triumphant in all its resplendent badness.

That book, *Grand Days,* was absolutely unpublishable. I knew the author of *The Warriors,* Sol Yurick, through a mutual friend, and he was kind enough to send it to his editor, Joyce Johnson — the same Joyce Johnson who wrote *Minor Characters* about her relationship with Jack Kerouac — after it had been rejected by numerous agents, editors and slush-pile readers. She sent me a nice little note attached to the manuscript basically telling me and my unlovely writing to get lost. I can take a hint as well as the next guy, so I decided to kill my book. I mean, it wasn't only the rejection slips that pushed me in this direction. By now, even a fellow as dense as myself realized how poorly I'd behaved in my marriage, and that I should have put more value on it than on my unintelligible excuse of a novel. So, to free myself from a host of bad memories and even worse decisions, I shoveled the pages down a storm grate in Manhattan after work on a rainy fall evening in 1975, hoping they'd somehow find their way to the Great Conductor's lair. Larry McMurtry, in *All of My Friends are Going to be Strangers,* drowns his manuscript in the Rio Grande. A wonderful and perfect ending to that novel. But there is the possibility that his main character dies while doing this, so perhaps his book was worse than mine.

Bill Anthony

The Bust

Years ago I got fired from a shitty low-paying job at the Strand Bookstore — but it was for a crime I didn't commit. I was working the cash register in the front of the store, and noticed an expensive leather-bound set of Dickens' letters, wrapped in brown paper, on the counter in front of me. I figured it had been sent down from the rare books room on the fifth floor and was waiting for a customer to come in and pick it up. It was an extremely slow day, so I started doodling with a ballpoint pen on the wrapping.

From out of nowhere, two hands appeared, grabbed at the parcel and tried to snatch it from the counter. I held it in place and looked up to see what was going on. I was surprised to find myself staring at the face of an ex-employee. This particular ex-employee was a strange dude from the Midwest who wore size-17 Converse, and resembled Civil War soldiers I'd seen in old photographs. I sometimes thought that if reincarnation was real, that's what he had been.

And he *was* a thief — a very clever thief. He was in charge of taking books that had been ordered by mail to the post office on Fourth Avenue, and paying to have them shipped to out-of-state customers. On one of his trips he'd reached into a postal clerk's window when his back was turned, and scooped up a receipt book. He would pay, let's say, fifty dollars for a mailing, write seventy-five on his own copy of the receipt, tossing away the real one, and pocket the difference. He'd then wheel his mail cart over to the Albert Hotel on University Place where he lived, park it outside, take a bunch of books he hadn't paid for up to his room, and then return to the store. He was efficient, so only a few of us knew what he was up to and, as we weren't snitches, nobody told on him. More to the point; he was very strong, and very crazy, and those are the real reasons nobody spilled the beans. He was finally let go because one of the managers sort of suspected something, or just because he was so weird.

Anyway, he glared at me and told me he was taking the Dickens.

"Man, you can't do that! That's stealing! I'll get fired!"

"Oh, alright! Here you go," he said, tossing a crumpled-up ten dollar bill over the counter, where it fell to the floor. When I bent over to pick it up, he grabbed the package and left.

It turned out that the manager who had gotten him fired had been tailing him, witnessed the entire transaction, and thought I was in cahoots with the thief. So I got fired; no matter how much I protested and tried to explain what had really happened.

I filed for unemployment, but was told that my former employer was blocking any payments. I panicked; I was living pretty close to the edge, and the store wasn't paying me all that much as it was — I sure hadn't managed to save anything. I figured I might be able set things straight by getting the books back to the store. I took a couple of friends along in case things got physical and went over to the Albert Hotel. My friends kept out of sight in the stairwell while I banged on his door.

Much to my surprise, he opened the door and let me in. His room was unfurnished — there was just this massive pile of books and boxes in the center of the floor, which was bare. There seemed to be some kind of sleeping bag next to it with a blanket strewn on top. I looked around, still kind of surprised to be there, and noticed that there was a mantel on the wall to the right of the door over a fake fireplace, with stuff on it — some candles and what looked like a bust. I walked over for a closer look and discovered that it was a black marble bust of Adolf Hitler. I mumbled something or another about my financial situation, and how desperate I was, but I couldn't focus; I was shaking. He seemed to sense my extreme unease, and must have felt sorry for me, because he gave me back the Dickens, still wrapped in the brown paper covered with my doodles.

I clutched the package and staggered out into the hallway feeling like I'd been punched in the chest by a massive dark fist.

Larry Deyab

Man in the Grey Flannel Beret

(Thanx and a tip of the hat to Mike Golden)

In the early 70's I was a stoned-out hippy working in a bookstore on the Lower East Side of Manhattan. I had long hair, a peace sign dangling from a leather lanyard around my neck and a dog-eared copy of *Howl* in my back pocket. Luckily for me, the bookstore job was pretty low key. Sometimes, on really slow nights, we'd close the cash register and have poetry readings.

One warm summer evening Allen Ginsberg read there. After the reading, Ginsberg invited us to accompany him to a bar for some beers.

Man, I got so excited! I was finally going to hear first-hand those rumored stories about wild fucking in freight cars, drug-crazed nights in exotic Mexican jungles and gay hustling on the Four-O-Deuce. I lit a joint and eagerly followed the poet across the street to the Centre Pub. But the conversation didn't go at all the way I thought it would.

Ginsberg proceeded to minutely detail for our enjoyment his book and record deals — how many tenths of a cent he got per copy of *Howl* sold. The only interesting moment occurred when Ginsberg interrupted himself to shout: *"Who the fuck is Maynard G. Krebs, anyway?"*

I got thoroughly drunk and left; disappointed, but still loving my beat-up copy of *Howl* — Allen had signed it, and then drawn a cartoon of a flower under his signature before we left the store.

***

By the mid-80's I was working in a different bookstore on St. Mark's Place. I had a buzz-cut, and wore a black leather jacket. Ginsberg's *Collected Poems* had just been published in an expensive hardcover edition, and we were doing a brisk business with the red dust jacketed item.

The store's owner gave me Ginsberg's phone number and told me to call him and ask him to stop by and sign copies of his book. Books signed by their authors usually sell faster than unsigned ones — they're simply more valuable. I said ok, and when I had a spare moment I dialed the number. Ginsberg answered — that was my first surprise — I'd expected an answering machine, or some kind of intermediary.

"Hi, Mr. Ginsberg," I said. "Is there any chance you could come by the bookstore and sign copies of your new book?"

"Sure," he said, "but only if you can tell me exactly how many copies have sold."

"I don't know," I answered truthfully, somewhat taken aback.

"Well, you'd better find out," he said, "if you want to see me any time in the near future."

"Just a minute — I'll ask the boss," I said in a panic, knowing I'd be in deep shit if I fucked this up. The guy I worked for really got off on thinking he was respected by the local literary heavyweights. If Ginsberg didn't show up, it would be such a blow to his ego he'd have me sweeping the floors and dusting the shelves for the rest of my shift.

I put my hand over the receiver and asked the other clerks if anyone knew exactly has many copies of Ginsberg's *Collected Poems* we'd already sold. Nobody had a clue. I took my hand off the receiver and said, "Fifty."

"Great," he said. "I'll be right over."

Ken Brown

Damaged Goods

"*Sonofabitch!* Get the *fuck* out of my cab!" drifts through the open third floor window, waking me up. Damn, it's probably my downstairs neighbor, Mitzi, returning home after another night out. She consumes amazing amounts of alcohol to blot out the pain she's in. She suffers from osteoporosis; her muscles and ligaments atrophying as well. The only way she's able to ambulate at all is by using numerous braces and splints: small ones on her arms, large ones on her legs, a corset-thing for her spine. Plus she's got a complete set of dentures, which she pops in and out to get the occasional laugh, and one glass eye. To complete the picture, she must weigh close to 300 pounds. Her brace-like contraptions are essentially tiny dams holding a tremendous lake in place. She's usually still sober enough at closing time to make it into a cab where she immediately unstraps and unhooks them, probably heaving a huge sigh of relief as she does so. The moment they're all undone her shapeless body flows like unchecked lava into every crevice of the back seat and she passes out. I totally sympathize with the frantic cabbie, whose angry voice I can still hear, and wonder how he explained this situation to his dispatcher.

"Pockita-pockita, Brooklyn Bridge, squatch-squatch, wrap-it-up!"

Great. Eduardo, who lives in the first floor front apartment, must be awake too. Eduardo is a small dark man from Panama. He has salt and pepper hair—mostly salt. Smoke and fire are his elements. He disconnected the old gas stove in his kitchen, removed the jets and burners, and filled the resulting cavity with charcoal which smolders day and night, creating a dense black cloud. We called the fire department more than once after he moved in, but they said there's nothing they can do, so we've learned to live with it.

If his element is smoke, his expertise is cunnilingus. He has set, he assures me, an official record of two hours and forty minutes while doing it. His entire stock of broken English expressions revolves around that particular part of the female anatomy and his special relationship with it. "Windshield wiper," he'll say, elbowing me, or "Brooklyn Bridge." Sometimes it's "going to the basement" but most of the time he calls it "swimming."

I know I'm not going to get any sleep unless I help the cabbie get Mitzi out of his car and into her apartment. I pull on my pants and slippers and head for the street. As I pass by his door, Eduardo throws it open, smoke billowing around him like a stage effect, shouting "I'm gonna break my nose! Wrap-it-up!" and leers in my general direction. His glasses are fogged—spirals of smoke rise from his sweater. He places his forefingers and thumbs together, so that they seem to form a crude vagina, and sticks his enormous meaty tongue through the result, wagging it up and down.

"Chewcha!" he cackles.

"Eduardo, you are a sexist pig," I say, trying to wave him back into his apartment.

"Chung-doom-bloom," he sniggers, retreating.

Somehow the cabbie, who's a big guy, and I manage to drag Mitzi out of the car and into the building where we deposit her in front of her apartment door. The driver goes back out and brings in an armload of splints and her purse, which he drops next to her inert form. He then gratefully exits, having collected his fare in advance. Now there's only the little problem of rousing Mitzi and making sure she gets safely inside her flat. Not a moot point as Eduardo materializes in the hallway in a puff of smoke like a sooty genie. He proceeds to dance around Mitzi's supine body, pointing out the, by now all too obvious, fact that her legs are spread wide open and she seems to be lacking any undergarments, which drives him into an absolute frenzy.

"Toonyfish! Chewchal I'm gonna go to de basement and break my record! Two-to-one!"

"Damn it!" I hiss, grabbing him by the shirt and shaking him to break the spell. "Please get back in your apartment, Eduardo—this isn't helping things!"

I push him away from Mitzi and clumsily try to rearrange the voluminous folds of her skirt in such a way as to cover her exposed parts.

"Mitzi, please wake up. Mitzi, I need your help. Mitzi, where are your keys? Mitzi, this is a nightmare!"

But I'm not having any luck with this approach so, ignoring my qualms, I open her battered purse, dumping the contents on the floor: a grimy lipstick tube, a cracked compact, a couple of sticks of gum and numerous prescription vials—but no keys—must've left them at the bar.

I push Eduardo into his apartment and tell him I'll call the cops if he so much as peeks in the hall. I sprint outside the building to the basement grates in the front sidewalk. They're never locked, so I pull one side open and descend into blackness. I have a plan, though I have to admit I'm kind of apprehensive about pulling it off, but I don't seem to have any choice; Mitzi's way too heavy to hoist up the two flights to my apartment and I don't have the vaguest idea where I'd put her if I was able to. I sleep on a small sofa bed—no other furniture. My studio apartment is filled with books; some of them on shelves but most of them in boxes, or in piles on top of the boxes. I can't help it; I work in a bookstore. I'm a hoarder, a collector. I simply have to get Mitzi into her own place, and that's why I'm heading into the unknown, figuring that the basement has to extend the entire length of the building and that I should be able to climb out the other end into some sort of backyard, where I'll try to break into one of Mitzi's bedroom windows and then unlock her door. If everything works out.

The basement has an incredibly low overhead. I scuttle along in the darkness, practically bent in half, brushing aside wires and old clotheslines. I feel a string in front of me and pull it. A dim 40-watt bulb snaps on, illuminating a large, squat boiler, a slop sink, and a jumble of ancient tools lying on the crumbling cement floor. Everything is covered with dust and cobwebs. There's an old baby crib in the way, which I push aside. Just past it, I stumble upon a worn flight of steps leading up to another set of grates. I shove one side open and emerge into an overgrown junk heap: mounds of rotting lumber, a broken washing machine, torn plastic garbage bags filled with decaying food, everything surrounded by tall weeds.

I roll the washing machine over to the back wall of the building and by standing on it I'm just able to reach one of Mitzi's rear windows. I have the eerie feeling that one of the neighbors in an adjacent building is watching me and is even now calling the police. I'll end up in jail and Mitzi will continue to lie in the hallway, unconscious, and Eduardo will eventually realize that he can have his way with her.

I break a bottom pane, reach inside and unlock the window. I'm able to raise it just enough to squeeze through. Tumbling down into darkness I crash into some sort of knick-knack table, scattering small breakable things everywhere. I finally locate a wall switch, turn it on and look around. Mitzi's apartment is all large pieces of furniture covered with shiny plastic slipcovers.

I unlock the door and, using all my strength, I pull her humongous insensate body in. I try to prop her on an overstuffed sofa, but she keeps sliding down onto the floor. I wedge her in place by jamming a coffee table against her left side and the TV cabinet against the other.

I put a pot of water on to boil and rummage through her crowded cabinets looking for instant coffee. I'm almost beginning to relax. It's only 4:30 in the morning. Maybe I'll even get back to sleep before the night is over.

In fact, Mitzi seems to be snapping out of her stupor. As I return from the kitchen with a steaming cup of coffee she opens her one good eye and stares up at me.

"Where am I? Ronald, is that you? Where's Eduardo? He's usually here by now!"

And that does it for me. I say good-night, leaving her apartment door open and knock on Eduardo's. When he opens it, I head for the stairway.

Bob Eckstein

Ugly George

Back in the day, when cable TV was brand new, there was a guy with a local show who called himself "Ugly George." And it's true; he wasn't very attractive. He had a sweaty tangle of black stringy hair, a squirrelly look, and his portable camera was a battered piece of crap; all wrapped in tape.

Anyway, Ugly George would cruise the city looking for attractive women. His territory was the back streets, where there wasn't a lot of foot traffic to contend with. When he found one, he'd approach her and ask if she would remove her top and show him, and by extension his audience, her tits. Most said "no." but every now and again he got lucky. I thought he was a slimy sexist pig, and I detested him.

One day he wandered into Coliseum Books, the store I was working in at the time, and he approached one of the cashiers in the front of the store. I lost it. I rolled up my T-shirt and walked briskly up to him.

"Hey, you big piece of shit, what do you think of these?" I snarled, shaking my bare chest.

"Don't do this to me!" he cried, turning and fleeing the store.

I chased him up Broadway, rubbing my nipples. I can't tell you how good the cool air felt on them.

Clayton Patterson

Fate Conspires a Perfect Joke

I was walking across 57th street on my way to work when I noticed him up ahead scuffling along the curb—silver hair, blue jacket and white sneakers. I probably wouldn't have given him a second thought, but he reminded me of someone I know from the literary scene. As I pulled even, I realized I'd been mistaken. His hair was dirty yellow, unwashed, and one look at the shoes clinched it; worn-out sneakers whispering, "Street, street." The guy was probably homeless. Fucked-up world, I thought, and swung into the front door of the bookstore.

Later, I met Jim Feast for dinner at a neighborhood deli. We were in the middle of fixing up a manuscript, and the give-and-take had been a lot of fun. We bought sandwiches and coffees and headed for a back booth. And then I saw him again, sitting at a small table, head cradled in his arms, zonked out. A large Coke teetered precariously near his elbow, and sure enough, the next thing you know he'd knocked it to the floor, where the reddish-brown liquid puddled like blood. Poor fucker, I thought, and then poor fuckers for the counter guys who were going to have to mop up the mess.

So Jim and I got down to business, ripping out words and telescoping paragraphs—beating a piece of writing into shape. And then, from out of nowhere, like a state trooper screaming through your car window when you're pumping away in the back seat, he's in our face yelling at us to "Buy me a sandwich buy me a drink give me money heal my wounds," slinging spittle on my fucking glasses.

"Jesus," I say to the dude, "We're trying to have a conversation here—get ahold of yourself!" but he's cursing and windmilling his arms in every which direction like a helicopter going down.

"Back off!" I shout at him, but it's like I'm not really there. And then I get a thought — a truly inspired stupid thought—a thought I've carried around in the tattered knapsack that is my brain for oh so long. You see, I kinda look like a Vietnam vet. I've got long stringy hair and a gray mustache, and I'm certainly old enough to have gone, though I didn't because I didn't want to kill anyone back then—or now, for that matter. Anyway, I figured if some young buck jumped me some dark night I'd act flipped-out Nam-style and rant that I'd offed tons of geeks and I'd do him, too. But I'd never had to go there—till now. So I shout, "I fuckin' killed guys in Nam and cut their ears off and strung 'em on a necklace, so get the fuck out of my face!"

Whoa, and the dude stops dead still, rolls up a sleeve exposing a bony arm, Auschwitz thin, with a tattoo of some kind of parachute device on it and says, "Brother, I was there, too. 82nd Airborne. You?" And I'm floored once again by how the heavens work and how big an ass-hole I am, and I'm wondering what the fuck I'm gonna say to this fella, but it's all moot. The dude wanders back to his table and passes out again. The drama's over and I'm left with an indefinite period of time in which to appreciate the Great Playwright's amazing sense of humor.

Jeffrey Isaac

The Collector

I'm a collector. I hunt down runs of literary magazines and signed first editions, and place them in university library archives. I collect comic books and the Jokers from decks of playing cards. I also lust after die-cast model cars; mostly Hot Wheels. I have hundreds of them — maybe thousands — some on display, but most of them stashed away in boxes.

As I've gotten older, it's become more difficult to compete with younger Hot Wheels collectors. They line-up outside the doors at Toys R Us and, when the store opens, they shove the mothers with their kids aside as they race to see who can get to the pegs first. I usually come in last. So, in order to get the newest releases I've had to hook up with a "dealer" — a guy who spends most of his waking hours tracking down product; some for himself, some to list on eBay, and the rest for schmucks like myself.

My dealer's name is Ken, and he's a prison guard who works the night shift at Rikers, which means he just barely makes it to the store before it opens. But he's buff, so no one fucks with him — he always gets to the Hot Wheels display rack first without having to hustle — the other collectors part like the Red Sea when he walks by.

Anyway, I took the day off from work and made plans to meet him on the Toys R Us parking lot in Long Island City on the morning of September eleventh, 2001. My wife and I sent our two sons off to school and then walked across Northern Boulevard towards the store. His car was parked pretty far away from the entrance, even though the lot was mostly empty. We noticed as we approached that his car doors were open, and his car was surrounded by several young girls all wearing red t-shirts, who seemed to be listening to the car radio, which was turned up real loud. Then we saw in the distance a plume of smoke rising into the sky from the city's skyline; more specifically, from one of the World Trade Center towers.

"Seems to have been hit by a small plane," Ken told us when we got to his car.

"Man, New York City firemen are the best," I enthused. "They're probably inside putting it out right now."

Moments later a manager came charging out of the store, shouting, "I don't give a fuck what's going on! If you don't get your asses inside and punch in I'll fire all of you!" which quickly dispersed the crowd.

I looked back at the skyline — one of the towers had disappeared and smoke was now pouring out of what used to be its twin. When we heard on the radio that planes were flying into things, my wife left to get our youngest son, while I flagged down a car service to Astoria to collect our oldest.

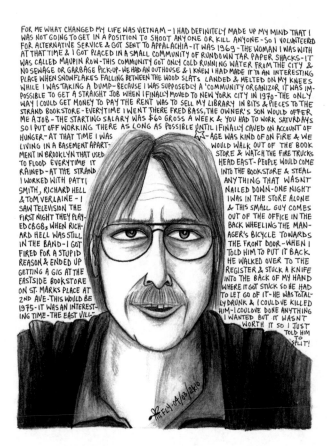

FOR ME WHAT CHANGED MY LIFE WAS VIETNAM – I HAD DEFINITELY MADE UP MY MIND THAT I WAS NOT GOING TO GET IN A POSITION TO SHOOT ANYONE OR KILL ANYONE – SO I VOLUNTEERED FOR ALTERNATIVE SERVICE & GOT SENT TO APPALACHIA – IT WAS 1969 – THE WOMAN I WAS WITH AT THAT TIME & I GOT PLACED IN A SMALL COMMUNITY OF RUNDOWN TAR PAPER SHACKS – IT WAS CALLED MAUPIN ROW – THIS COMMUNITY GOT ONLY COLD RUNNING WATER FROM THE CITY & NO SEWAGE OR GARBAGE PICK-UP – WE HAD AN OUTHOUSE & I KNEW I HAD MADE IT TO AN INTERESTING PLACE WHEN SNOWFLAKES FALLING BETWEEN THE WOOD SLATS LANDED & MELTED ON MY KNEES WHILE I WAS TAKING A DUMP – BECAUSE I WAS SUPPOSEDLY A 'COMMUNITY ORGANIZOR' IT WAS IMPOSSIBLE TO GET A STRAIGHT JOB WHEN I FINALLY MOVED TO NEW YORK CITY IN 1970 – THE ONLY WAY I COULD GET MONEY TO PAY THE RENT WAS TO SELL MY LIBRARY IN BITS & PIECES TO THE STRAND BOOKSTORE – EVERYTIME I WENT THERE FRED BASS, THE OWNER'S SON WOULD OFFER ME A JOB – THE STARTING SALARY WAS $60 GROSS A WEEK & YOU HAD TO WORK SATURDAYS SO I PUT OFF WORKING THERE AS LONG AS POSSIBLE UNTIL I FINALLY CAVED ON ACCOUNT OF HUNGER – AT THAT TIME I WAS

LIVING IN A BASEMENT APART-
MENT IN BROOKLYN THAT USED
TO FLOOD EVERYTIME IT
RAINED – AT THE STRAND
I WORKED WITH PATTI
SMITH, RICHARD HELL
& TOM VERLAINE – I
SAW TELEVISION THE
FIRST NIGHT THEY PLAY-
ED CBGBs WHEN RICH-
ARD HELL WAS STILL
IN THE BAND – I GOT
FIRED FOR A STUPID
REASON & ENDED UP
GETTING A GIG AT THE
EASTSIDE BOOKSTORE
ON ST. MARKS PLACE AT
2ND AVE – THIS WOULD BE
1975 – IT WAS AN INTEREST-
ING TIME – THE EAST VILL-

–AGE WAS KIND OF ON FIRE & WE
WOULD WALK OUT OF THE BOOK
STORE & WATCH THE FIRE TRUCKS
HEAD EAST – PEOPLE WOULD COME
INTO THE BOOKSTORE & STEAL
ANYTHING THAT WASN'T
NAILED DOWN – ONE NIGHT
I WAS IN THE STORE ALONE
& THIS SMALL GUY COMES
OUT OF THE OFFICE IN THE
BACK WHEELING THE MAN-
AGER'S BICYCLE TOWARDS
THE FRONT DOOR – WHEN I
TOLD HIM TO PUT IT BACK
HE WALKED OVER TO THE
REGISTER & STUCK A KNIFE
INTO THE BACK OF MY HAND
WHERE IT GOT STUCK SO HE HAD
TO LET GO OF IT – HE WAS TOTAL-
LY DRUNK & I COULD'VE KILLED
HIM – I COULD'VE DONE ANYTHING
I WANTED BUT IT WASN'T
WORTH IT SO I JUST
TOLD HIM
TO
SPLIT!

Fly

About the Author

RON KOLM is a founding member of the Unbearables and one of the editors of their anthologies. He is also a contributing editor of *Sensitive Skin* magazine. Ron is the author of *The Plastic Factory, Divine Comedy*, *Suburban Ambush* and, with Jim Feast, the novel *Neo Phobe*. A new collection of his short stories, *Duke & Jill*, has just been published by Unknown Press. He's had work in *Hobo Camp Review, Have A NYC 3,* the *Too Much* anthology, *The Otter* and *the Outlaw Bible of American Poetry.* Ron's papers were purchased by the New York University library, where they've been catalogued in the Fales Collection as part of the Downtown Writers Group.

The Worst Book I Ever Read
The Unbearables

Over 400 pages of the most searing, scandalous and scurrilous denunciations of fellow writers ever to appear in print! Innovative, free-form and traditional reviews of texts from the Bible and *Ulysses* to Borges, Calvino and David Sedaris by Luc Sante, Peter Lamborn Wilson, Jim Knipfel, Carl Watson, David Ulin, Sharon Mesmer, many more. Many color illus. ISBN:9781570271991 412pp. 6"x9" $16.95

Negativeland A Novel
Doug Nufer

In this rueful tale, written under a simple but pervasive formal constraint, Olympic gold medal winner Ken Honochick and his girlfriend take a cross-country road trip to revisit his brief moment of triumph and his subsequent long haul on the promotions circuit. The result is a smart, flirtatious tour-de-force that's as funny as it is inventive. Under all the comic gusto and technical virtuosity, however, there's also some penetrating thought on our country's obsession with private foibles and public image, individual achievement and the pressure to cash in on it. ISBN:1570271593 192pp. 4½"x7" $9.95

Neo Phobe A Novel
Jim Feast with Ron Kolm

A serial rapist terrorizes the streets of New York City, forcing a low-rent group of freelancers to go head-to-head with a Fundamentalist-Industrial Complex in a race to solve crimes. "*Neo Phobe* aims directly at the paradox that lies at the center of all sexual liberatory writing. Often it suggests brilliant resolutions of this paradox; sometimes it falls victim to it. Everyone should read this book." —Samuel Delany. ISBN: 1570271712 256pp. $12.95

Crimes of the Beats
The Unbearables

One evening, the Unbearables were bemoaning the sorry state of radical culture, and asked themselves what single act they could do to release themselves from their past, while at the same time honoring it. Perhaps put the beatniks, the real beatniks, on trial? Turn the Crimes of the Beats into the Nuremberg of Bohemia: Call out Burroughs for copping W. C. Fields' act, and Ginsberg for being the original Maynard G. Krebs in the gray flannel beret—always hyping, hyping, hyping the myth, then selling, selling, selling it as the only viable alternative to the polluted mainstream. And of course Jackie boy himself for claiming that he wrote On the Road in one sitting, a lie that ruined three whole generations of novelists gobbling speed to duplicate the feat of the beat that never really went down in anything short of seven drafts. File under "Literary Criticism." ISBN:1570270694 224pp. 6"x9" $14.95

The Ass's Tale A Novel
John Ferris

A Rabelaisian story of a dog's search for his identity. Told in the existential down-and-dirty vein of Ralph Ellison, Ishmael Reed and Chester Himes, as this manuscript circulated in New York City's Lower East Side, it became legendary. "Hot dog! Dirty dog! If you ever wanted to know about invisible sex, check this out!" Steve Cannon ISBN: 9781570272219 208pp.   6"x9" $15.95

Shorts Are Wrong
Mike Topp

"Mike Topp's irreducible art consists partly of recycling expandable parts of speech and revealing their unused genius. Other parts are fixed, like the sly orthography. Topp is the Andy Warhol and Ralph Nader of literature." — Andrei Codrescu "Just when I think Mike Topp's poems are funny, they're wise. Just when I think they're wise, they're bad. Just when I think they're bad, they're great. Mike Topp's book is exactly like the world." — Eileen Myles
ISBN: 9781570271861 128pp.   4½"x7" $9.95

Help Yourself!
The Unbearables

Hilarious and outrageous send-ups of self-help literature by Samuel R. Delaney, Robert Anton Wilson, Sparrow, Jim Knipfel, Arthur Nersesian, Bob Holman, Carl Watson, Doug Nufer, Richard Kostelanetz, Tsaurah Litzky, Denise Duhamel, Christian X. Hunter, Michael Carter, Jill Rapaport, Ron Kolm, many more.
ISBN:1570271046 192pp.   6"x9" $14.95

Hotel of Irrevocable Acts A Novel
Carl Watson

In the warped underworld of Uptown Chicago two petty thieves, Jack and Vince—Dostoevskyan in their criminal use of philosophy, exalting in the stealing of art as the highest human act—meet their target, their nemesis and their double: Madame Little-Ease, a Satanic Grandma Moses who paints on refuse with polluted blood. "Carl Watson is a true visionary and an artist of letters, who also happens to be a pure pleasure to read." — John Strausbaugh
ISBN: 9781570271762 160pp. 6"x9" $15.95

MORE UNBEARABLES TITLES FROM AUTONOMEDIA

Spermatogonia: The Isle of Man
Bart Plantenga

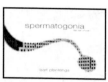

Psychogeography is the study of the effects of the geo-
graphic environment on the emotions and behavior of in-
dividuals. So when Kees Califlora, a corporate
psychogeographer (paid to locate places where people are
predisposed to certain marketable behaviors), begins to
doubt the validity of his own identity and experience, he's too well-informed about the
fictions of his own life to address it directly. The result is a dizzy unravelling, as Kees
abandons friendships, interactions, and eventually even language.
ISBN:1570271607 144pp. 4½"x7" $7.95

The Unbearables First Anthology
The Unbearables

Fictive adventures by the Unbearables and collaborators, a free-
floating in-your-face scrum of black humorists, chaos-mongers, im-
mediatists, and verse-spouting Beer Mystics©, disorganized around
recuperating essence away from the humorless commodification of
experience. Includes: Judy Nylon, Max Blagg, Bikini Girl, Bruce Ben-
derson, Hakim Bey, Jordan Zinovich, dozens more.
ISBN: 1570270538 288pp. 6"x9" $14.95

This Young Girl Passing A Novel
Donald Breckenridge

This Young Girl Passing explores the dynamics of an illicit relationship between a troubled schoolgirl and her young French teacher in
Upstate NY in the 1970s, simultaneously capturing the feel of post-
Vietnam life in America. In alternating chapters the novel jumps
twenty years forward, tracing the renewed affair between the teacher
and student (by then married with a teenage daughter of her own)
which continues until the teacher's wife discovers the affair. This
Young Girl Passing is a non-linear love story and a realistic portrayal of Middle America
that spans three decades. ISBN: 9781570272349 144pp. 6"x9" $12.95

Rat Hunt Boys A Novel
Anna Mockler

"The perfect story to read aloud either to your elders or youngsters,
whomever is stranger. If the Rutabaga Stories are overcooked and
the Brothers Grimm's aren't grim enough, try a trip to this Pepperland
of absurdities. If language is a virus, as Burroughs has put it, this
strain of pidgin is mutantly vaccine resistant, bubonic in its intensity;
a queerly affecting tale of creatures ravaged by apocalyptic misad-
venture." — Kevin Riordan
ISBN: 9781570273100 448pp. 6"x9" $18.95